DISNEY's Beauty AND THE BEAST THE ENCHANTED CHRISTMAS

A
MOUSE WORKS
MOVIE STORYBOOK

Christmas is a magical time, but nowhere was it more magical than at the Beast's castle. The dark and gloom were gone forever. Belle's love for the Beast had changed everything, and now all of the enchanted objects were people again—including little Chip!

On his first Christmas as a real boy, Chip had one special request. "Please, Mama," Chip begged, "tell the story of what happened last Christmas!"

"Well," Mrs. Potts said as she settled herself into a chair, "Belle had been the Master's guest for a while, and we were beginning to hope that she would be the one to break the spell…

But the Beast wasn't making it easy. He was a grump, even at Christmas. And I suppose he had his reasons."

"It was at Christmas that I was changed from a prince into this horrible beast! I hate Christmas!" the Beast roared to Forte, the pipe organ. Fife, the piccolo, watched the Beast rant and rave. He dared not make a sound when the Beast was so upset.

You see, Forte, the former court composer, was the Beast's sole confidante. Of all the enchanted objects, he was the only one who never wanted to be human again. Forte knew that his somber music would have a place in the Beast's heart as long as the Beast remained unhappy.

Belle didn't know why the Beast hated Christmas. She just thought he liked being miserable. Wanting to change that, she decided to surprise the Beast with a Christmas celebration.

I got busy cooking a feast. Others gathered mistletoe, garlands, and tinsel. Then Belle and Lumiere went up into the attic in search of the lovely Angelique, the Christmas tree angel, and the other ornaments.

When Angelique heard about the plans for a Christmas celebration, she got very upset. She knew that the Beast would never allow Christmas in the castle. The only thing she and the ornaments had to look forward to was disappointment once again.

Despite Angelique's concerns, everyone's hard work turned the castle into something quite magical. The air was filled with the sweet scent of pine garlands. Ornaments twinkled and glittered in the candlelight.

Belle felt just one more thing was needed to make it perfect—a yule log for Christmas wishes. So she went down to the boiler room to fetch one. But just as Belle found the perfect log, the Beast stormed into the room! Snatching the log from Belle he thundered, "There will be no Christmas!"

Belle refused to give up hope. "We'll have Christmas with or without him!" she declared.

But Forte had other plans for Belle.

When Belle could not
find a perfect Christmas
tree on the castle grounds,
Forte deviously suggested
that she search the Black
Forest for one.

"But I promised the
Beast I would never leave
the castle grounds," said
Belle. "I gave my word."

"Have it your way," said the
evil Forte. "But the Master
does love Christmas trees."

That was all Belle needed
to hear! Determined to have
Christmas, Belle set out
to search for the perfect
tree. Chip was so excited,
he nearly pushed her out
the door. Forte insisted that
the reluctant Fife follow
along. It was all part of
his wicked plan!

As soon as Belle had left the castle, the Beast decided he wanted to see her. But Belle was nowhere to be found. Gazing into his enchanted mirror, the Beast saw her riding away in a sleigh!

"I didn't think she would leave," said the Beast sadly.

"She's abandoned you," hissed Forte. "She only wanted this Christmas nonsense to distract you so she could escape!"

"I'll bring her back!" yelled the Beast.

Then he stormed through the castle, destroying everything— the ornaments, the tinsel, the garlands, and the beautiful holiday table which Angelique had helped decorate. Sadly, Angelique realized that she had been right all along. Once again, there would be no Christmas in the castle.

Forte wanted Belle destroyed, for he knew that if she made the Master happy there would be no need for him and his sad music. So he told his faithful sidekick, Fife, to make sure that Belle never returned from the forest.

Fife didn't really want to hurt Belle, but when he suddenly appeared at her side in the middle of the woods, his piping frightened Phillipe. The horse jumped back in fear, sending the sleigh and Chip into the frozen river. Belle jumped in and saved Chip, but then she was swept under the ice!

That's when the Beast appeared! He plunged into the freezing water and pulled Belle out!

The Beast saved Belle and carried her back to the castle. There he locked her away in the dungeon. "You broke your word," he growled.

Sad, lonely, and defeated, the Beast returned to his room. There he found a Christmas gift from Belle. It was a book she had written just for him. Opening it carefully, the Beast began to read: *Once upon a time, there was an enchanted castle. This castle's master seemed as cold as winter. But deep inside his heart...*

It was only then that the Beast realized that Belle could see through his sadness and misery to the goodness he kept hidden inside.

The Beast hurried to the dungeon. "Belle, can you forgive me?" he asked.

"Of course." Belle smiled. "Merry Christmas."

But there was someone in the castle who was not having a very merry Christmas. When Forte saw that the Beast had befriended Belle, he swore revenge. Blasting his music throughout the castle, he made the walls quake and the stones tumble. He was trying to destroy the castle!

"Forte!" the Beast yelled as he ran upstairs to stop the jealous organ. But it was too late—the force of his own playing shattered Forte into a thousand pieces. Forte's sad music would be heard no more.

…When the dust and smoke had cleared," Mrs. Potts concluded, "everyone stood looking about. No one knew quite what to do. Finally the Beast spoke up. 'What are we standing around for?' he asked. 'Let's give Belle the Christmas she's always wanted!'

"The Beast opened the doors to a room decorated with the most beautiful Christmas tree. Belle would have Christmas at last. Lumiere nodded to Angelique, who took her place atop the tree.

"That Christmas was indeed a celebration to remember—especially for the Beast. Belle's gift to him that day was the gift of hope…a hope that someday the curse upon him would be lifted and life in the castle would begin anew."